ASTERIX
THE LEGIONARY

TEXT BY GOSCINNY

DRAWINGS BY UDERZO

TRANSLATED BY ROBERT STEVEN CARON

DARGAUD PUBLISHING INTERNATIONAL, LTD.

ASTERIX THE GAUL	0-917201-50-7
ASTERIX AND THE GOLDEN SICKLE	0-917201-64-7
ASTERIX AND THE GOTHS	0-917201-54-X
ASTERIX THE GLADIATOR	0-917201-55-8
ASTERIX AND THE BANQUET	0-917201-71-X
ASTERIX AND CLEOPATRA	0-917201-75-2
ASTERIX AND THE BIG FIGHT	0-917201-58-2
ASTERIX IN BRITAIN	0-917201-74-4
ASTERIX AND THE NORMANS	0-917201-69-8
ASTERIX THE LEGIONARY	0-917201-56-6
ASTERIX AND THE CHIEFTAIN'S SHIELD	0-917201-67-1
ASTERIX AT THE OLYMPIC GAMES	0-917201-61-2
ASTERIX AND THE CAULDRON	0-917201-66-3
ASTERIX IN SPAIN	0-917201-51-5
ASTERIX AND THE ROMAN AGENT	0-917201-59-0
ASTERIX IN SWITZERLAND	0-917201-57-4
ASTERIX AND THE MANSIONS OF THE GODS	0-917201-60-4
ASTERIX AND THE LAUREL WREATH	0-917201-62-0
ASTERIX AND THE SOOTHSAYER	0-917201-63-9
ASTERIX IN CORSICA	0-917201-72-8
ASTERIX AND CAESAR'S GIFT	0-917201-68-X
ASTERIX AND THE GREAT CROSSING	0-917201-65-5
OBELIX & CO.	0-917201-70-1
ASTERIX IN BELGIUM	0-917201-73-6

© DARGAUD EDITEUR PARIS 1967
© DARGAUD PUBLISHING INTERNATIONAL LTD. 1992
for the English language text

ISBN 0-917201-56-6

Exclusive licenced distributor for USA:

Distribooks Inc.
8220 N. Christiana Ave.
Skokie, IL 60076-2911
Tel: (708) 676-1596
Fax: (708) 676-1195
Toll-free fax: 800-433-9229

Imprimé en France-Publiphotoffset 93500 Pantin-en avril 1995

Printed in France

GAVLISH VILLAGE

DELIRIVM

NOHAPPIMEDIVM

AQVARIVM

OPPROBRIVM

A R M O R I C A

B E L G I C A

LVTETIA

SPQR

GAVL
(ROMAN CONQVEST)
50 B.C.

C E L T I C A

R O M A N
P R O V I N C I A

A Q V I T A N I A

The year is 50 B.C.   All of Gaul is occupied by the Romans.   All?   Not quite!   A village inhabited by the indomitable Gauls is holding out, strong as ever, against the invader.   Life is not easy for the Roman legionaries stationed in the fortified camps of Aquarium, Delirium, Nohappimedium and Opprobrium...

A FEW GAULS...

The hero of these adventures is Asterix. He is a cunning, quick-witted little warrior, so all the dangerous missions are automatically entrusted to him. Asterix owes his superhuman strength to the magic potion brewed by the Druid, Magigimmix...

Obelix is the side-kick of Asterix. He is a menhir delivery-man by trade, and relishes wild boar. Obelix is always ready to drop everything order to seek new adventures with Asterix... as long as the wild boar is plentiful and the fighting is rough...

Magigimmix, the venerable village druid, gathers mistletoe and concocts magic potions. His greatest discovery is the potion that confers superhuman strength on all who imbibe it. But Magigimmix has other recipes up his sleeve...

Malacoustix is the bard. Opinion is divided as to his talent. He thinks it is laudable, but everyone else finds it deplorable. However, as long as he keeps his mouth shut he is a jolly companion esteemed by all...

Finally, there is Macroeconomix, chief of the tribe. This majestic, courageous and touchy old warrior is respected by his men and feared by his enemies. Macroeconomix has just one fear – that the sky may fall on his head. But as he himself would say, "Fat chance!"

LATER...

THAT SURE WAS A GOOD HUNT, OBELIX.

HMMM?

LET'S COOK THE BOARS RIGHT AWAY AND THEN TAKE A LONG SNOOZE.

HEY, OBELIX! HOW ABOUT BRINGING THOSE BOARS?

HMMM. BOARS WHAT BOARS?

OH, RIGHT! THE BOARS.

GRRRAOORRR!

SHORTLY AFTERWARDS.

AAAH! THAT WAS YUMMY!

2A

OKAY, OBELIX! FINISH UP YOUR THIRD BOAR SO WE CAN TAKE A NAP. SCROTCH! SCRUTCH!

NO THANKS. I JUST DON'T FEEL HUNGRY ANY MORE. HEAVY SIGH

SCROTCH SCRUTCH!

OBELIX, IS SOMETHING THE MATTER?

NO, NO... HEAVIER SIGH

HEAVIEST SIGH

COME QUICKLY, O DRUID MAGIGIMMIX. I'M WORRIED ABOUT OBELIX. HE WON'T FINISH HIS BOAR AND HE SAYS HE'S NO LONGER HUNGRY.

DID HE EAT ANYTHING EARLIER?

JUST TWO BOARS

TWO MEASLY BOARS... THAT'S NOTHING. LET'S HAVE A LOOK AT HIM!

2B

7

9

I KNOW A SPOT NEAR THE TALL OAK WHERE THERE ARE HEAPS OF PRETTY FLOWERS, DELICATE, POETIC BLUE FLOWERS...

SOMEONE'S COMING, BY MERCURY! IT MAY BE THE GAULS. LET'S SEE IF WE CAN GET BY UNNOTICED.

OVER THERE! BY THAT TALL OAK!

I ... I THINK SOMEONE'S COMING THIS WAY!

ER ... QUOMODO VALES?

AREN'T YOU ASHAMED OF YOURSELVES TRAMPLING MY PRETTY BLUE FLOWERS?

AWFULLY SORRY... WE DIDN'T KNOW WE HAVE TO KEEP OFF THE ...

WHAM!

AND, AFTER GETTING RID OF THE INTRUDERS...

THE TROUBLE WITH YOU ROMANS IS THAT YOU'RE NEITHER DELICATE NOR POETIC.

AND THE TROUBLE WITH ME IS THAT I'M SO BASHFUL AND DISCREET!

SNIFF!

DID YOU HEAR WHAT THAT MASTODON SAID?

YEAH! THESE GAULS ARE CRAZY!

10

11

SNIFF!

HOW STRANGE, O MACROECONOMIX! WHY HAVE THE ROMANS BEGUN RECRUITING GAULS?

JULIUS CAESAR HAS PROBLEMS IN AFRICA WHERE HE'S FIGHTING THE ROMANS WHO BACK POMPEY...

HUH!

ACCORDING TO OUR LATEST REPORTS, HE'S BESIEGED IN RUSPINA.* HE NEEDS REINFORCEMENTS. HIS RECRUITING OFFICERS FIRST ASK FOR VOLUNTEERS AND IF THEY DON'T FIND ANY THEY TAKE THEM BY FORCE...

* MONASTIR (TUNISIA)

WE'LL GO AT ONCE TO CONDATUM TO TRY AND GET YOUNG TRAGICOMIX BACK BEFORE HE SAILS FOR AFRICA!

MY FRIENDS, I EXPECTED NOTHING LESS FROM YOU AND YOUR INDOMITABLE COURAGE! PHILHARMONIA'S FIANCÉ...

BOO HOO HOOO!

PREPARATIONS ARE QUICKLY MADE...

HERE'S SOME MAGIC POTION FOR YOU, ASTERIX...

THANK YOU, O DRUID MAGIGIMMIX!

SNIFF!

...AND THE TIME HAS COME TO SET OUT!

HOW CAN I EVEN THANK YOU?

YOU CAN THANK US WHEN WE BRING TRAGICOMIX BACK... AND THAT WE'LL DO UNLESS THE SKY FALLS ON OUR HEADS!

BE GOOD, DOGMATIX, I'LL BE BACK SOON...

PLEASE LOOK AFTER DOGMATIX, PHILHARMONIA.

I'LL TAKE GOOD CARE OF HIM, OBELIX... HE'S SO CUTE.

GRRR!

SMACK!

13

SO, I'M NOT GOING TO SING, EH?

NO, YOU ARE NOT GOING TO SING!

AND AFTER A BRIEF UNEVENTFUL JOURNEY...

NOW WE'VE GOT TO FIND THE ROMAN H.Q. AS SOON AS A LEGIONARY COMES BY WE'LL ASK HIM WHERE IT IS.

CONDATVM

AND, NEARBY, IN THE STREETS OF CONDATUM...

AVE!

YOU THERE! NO SALUTE FOR THE PATROL?

AVE!

YOU GOT AWAY WITH IT THIS TIME, BUT REMEMBER, ALWAYS SALUTE THE PATROL!

LOOK! THERE'S A PATROL! LET'S STOP IT AND...

RIGHT!

OBELIX! WAIT A SECOND!

A FEW MINUTES LATER...

ALL WE HAD TO DO WAS STOP THEM!

WELL, STOP THEM WE DID!

THERE ARE TIMES WHEN IT PAYS TO BE COURTEOUS, OBELIX...

WOULD YOU PLEASE BE SO KIND AS TO TELL US WHERE YOUR HEADQUARTERS ARE?

THIRD ON THE LEFT AND PLEASE DON'T SLUG ME ANY= MORE!

COURTESY OPENS DOORS, OBELIX...

AVE!

AH! HERE'S THE ROMAN LEGION HEADQUARTERS... WAIT FOR ME HERE; I DON'T TRUST YOU. WE HAVE TO BE COURTEOUS.

NO ENTRY! IF YOU WANT TO ENLIST, GAUL, YOU HAVE TO LINE UP LIKE THE OTHERS.

EXCUSE ME PLEASE... I'D JUST LIKE SOME INFORMATION.

LINE UP, I SAID!

THE PROBLEM IS, I'M IN A 'HURRY'!

THAT'S YOUR PROBLEM!

I'M GETTING HOT UNDER THE COLLAR... VERY HOT BY TOUTATIS!

BIFF!

I NEVER!...

I JUST DON'T SEE THE DIFFERENCE BETWEEN ASTERIX'S COURTESY AND MINE!

TCHAC!

WHERE CAN I FIND THE INFORMATION DESK, PLEASE?

WHO KNOWS? GO TO THE INFORMATION BUREAU. THEY'LL INFORM YOU.

15

AH, FINALLY!

COULD YOU PLEASE TELL ME IF YOU HAVE A LEGIONARY HERE BY THE NAME OF TRAGICOMIX?

QUIT THE POUNDING, FELONIUS, WE CAN'T HEAR OURSELVES SPEAK!

TAPTAPTAPTAP!

TO FIND THAT OUT YOU HAVE TO GO TO THE PERSONNEL OFFICE, FOURTH DOOR ON YOUR LEFT.

THE PERSONNEL OFFICE...

I'VE GOT FOUR CAESARS.

SPEAK TO THE CENTURION OF CALENDS, GAUL...

RING AROUND THE COLLAR, SHE ALWAYS USED TO HOLLAR...

WHAT YOU WANT IS THE INFORMATION BUREAU, BY JUPITER...

INFORMATION

I'VE HAD MY FILL OF THIS!

BANG!

ARE YOU GOING TO TELL ME WHERE TRAGICOMIX IS, YES OR NO?

BIFF! BIFF BIFF BIFF BIFF BIFF

TAPTAPTAPTAP!

QUIT THE POUNDING, GAUL, WE CAN'T HEAR OURSELVES THINK!

BIFF! BIFF! BIFF!

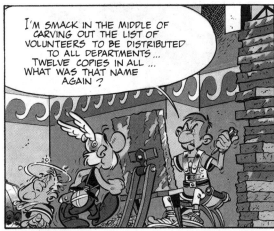

I'M SMACK IN THE MIDDLE OF CARVING OUT THE LIST OF VOLUNTEERS TO BE DISTRIBUTED TO ALL DEPARTMENTS... TWELVE COPIES IN ALL... WHAT WAS THAT NAME AGAIN?

TRAGICOMIX.

TRAGICOMIX... WITH A "T" AS IN TIMEO DANAOS AND DONA FERENTES?

WHY YES. HERE WE HAVE IT. TRAGICOMIX HAS LEFT WITH A CONVOY... AT THIS TIME HE MUST BE SETTING SAIL FROM MASSILIA WITH REINFORCEMENTS FOR CAESAR. THEY'RE HEADED FOR AFRICA.

AFRICA. HMMM.

OBELIX! COME HERE!

IS THAT YOU CALLING ASTERIX?

YES!

I'LL BE RIGHT THERE!

BUT FIRST, A LITTLE SHOW OF COURTESY.

WHAM!

?!!

TRAGICOMIX IS OFF TO AFRICA. THE ONLY WAY TO GET HIM BACK NOW IS TO JOIN THE ROMAN ARMY.

US? IN THE ROMAN ARMY?... WELL, IF YOU THINK IT COULD HELP PHILHARMONIA...

SHORTLY AFTERWARDS...

OOOOH... WHAT DID I EVER DO TO THOSE TWO?...

SO HERE ARE MY VOLUNTEERS! STEP RIGHT UP, BOYS! WELCOME!

WE DIDN'T SHOW MUCH COURTESY THIS TIME, ASTERIX.

ALL THINGS IN DUE TIME, OBELIX!

YOU'RE A-OK MY BOYS. NOW JUST TELL YOUR NAME TO THE LEGIONARY, HE'LL TAP OUT THE FORMS FOR YOU.

ANONYMOUS, GREEK POET, BY ZEUS!

VALUEADDED-TAX, BRITISH, I SAY!

DIETETIX, BELGIAN.

Chimeric, Gothic.

Metaforic, Gothic.

INTERPRETER?

CHIMERIC AND METAFORIC, BOTH GOTHS.

HE'S ASKING IF THIS IS REALLY AN INN?

TELL HIM IT IS AND GET HIS NAME FOR THE REGISTER.

PTIGHTNET.

ToC ToC ToC!

ASTERIX AND OBELIX, GAULS.

THAT SAYS IT ALL!

ToCToCToC!

QUIET! CUT THE GIGGLES, YOU'RE IN THE ARMY NOW!

HERE ARE THE NEW LEGIONARIES.

FINE. TELL THEM TO GET UNDRESSED!

U-UN-DRESS!

Undress!

Too skinny to be a legionary, he said!

I don't have enough padding he said!

THE EGYPTIAN SAYS HE'S AMAZED BY THE CUSTOMS OF GAULISH INNS...

I DON'T GIVE A HOOT! WE'RE GOING TO RENDER HIM UNTO CAESAR! EVERYONE OUT!

NOW GET DRESSED!

CAN'T YOU MAKE UP YOUR MIND?

THESE ROMANS ARE CRAZY!

What did the Gaul say?

He said the Centurion can't make up his mind!

WHO ASKED YOU TO TRANSLATE?

What did the Centurion say?

WHAT DID THE GOTH SAY?

OH, SO NOW YOU **WANT** ME TO TRANSLATE?

GNGNGNGNGNGNGNGN

LISTEN, WE'RE NOT HERE FOR A GOOD TIME. SO TELL US WHERE WE'RE SUPPOSED TO GO. LET'S SEE A BIT OF DISCIPLINE AROUND HERE.

THE EGYPTIAN WOULD LIKE TO SEE THE MENU.

SAY, DO YOU THINK THEY'LL HAVE BOAR?

DON'T COUNT ON IT! THE STRONGER THE ARMY, THE WORSE THE FOOD IS. THAT KEEPS THE MEN IN A FIGHTING MOOD!

SPLOTCH!

SPLOTCH!

SLURP

SPLOTCH!

I DIDN'T THINK THE ROMAN ARMY WAS THAT STRONG!

THE EGYPTIAN WOULD LIKE TO SEE THE MANAGER.

IF IT'S LIKE THIS, I REFUSE TO STAY FOR LESS THAN SIX SESTERTII!

BANG

THIS FOOD IS DEFINITELY LOW GOTHIC!

Where I come from you could be quartered for less!

SERIOUSLY, WHAT IS THIS ANYWAY?

IT'S YOUR COMMON EVERYDAY RATIONS: WHEAT, BACON AND CHEESE. WE COOK IT ALL TOGETHER TO SAVE TIME!

SUPPOSE WE HAD IT OUT WITH THE COOK, ASTERIX...

SLURP! SLURP!

YOU TOOK THE WORDS RIGHT OUT OF MY MOUTH, OBELIX!

DELICIOUS. SPLENDID. REALLY BRILLIANT, IS IT NOT?

? ? ? ? ? ?

26

ER... NOW FOR SOME GLADIUS PRACTICE...

OF COURSE, THESE ARE JUST MAKE BELIEVE SWORDS MADE OF WOOD.. LET'S GO!

?!

WELL, MOVE! DEFEND YOURSELF!

BUT IF IT'S JUST A WOODEN TOY...

JUST DO AS YOU'RE TOLD OBELIX! WE'RE WASTING TIME!

WELL ALL RIGHT THEN!

THESE ROMANS ARE CRAZY!

TCHAC!

OH NO! ENOUGH IS ENOUGH! IF THINGS GO ON LIKE THIS, IT'LL NEVER BE READY AND IT'LL TASTE MIGHTY FOUL!

23A

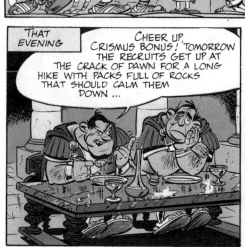

THAT EVENING

CHEER UP, CRISMUS BONUS! TOMORROW THE RECRUITS GET UP AT THE CRACK OF DAWN FOR A LONG HIKE WITH PACKS FULL OF ROCKS. THAT SHOULD CALM THEM DOWN ...

A NIP OF MAGIC POTION FOR TOMORROW, AND THEN TO BED. WE HAVE TO GET UP EARLY!

HOW ABOUT SOME MORE BOAR!

IN A JIFFY!

THAT'S RIGHT! THEY WON'T LOOK SO CLEVER TOMORROW WHEN I SHAKE THEM OUT OF BED AT DAWN!

BUT JUST A FEW SHORT HOURS LATER...

COME ON! EVERYBODY UP, UP, UP!

?

ON YOUR TOES EVERYONE!

LET'S GO EVERYONE!

IN A JI-JIFFY!

23B

UNDER THE COMMAND OF CENTURION LINGUAE LAPSUS, THE MEN OF THE 1ST LEGION, 3RD COHORT, 2ND MANIPLE, 1ST CENTURY LEAVE CONDATUM...

I THINK WE'VE BEEN MARCHING LONG ENOUGH. LET'S TAKE A BREAK

1ST LEGION, 3RD COHORT, 2ND MANIPLE, 1ST CENTURY, HALT! WE'RE TAKING A BREAK!

THE FASTER WE FIND TRAGICOMIX THE BETTER FOR PHIL= HARMONIA

I DON'T WANT PHILHARMONIA TO WORRY...

DO YOU THINK WE'LL FIND TRAGI= COMIX EASILY?

LET'S HOPE SO, OBELIX!

HEY! YOU TWO! I SAID WE'RE TAKING A BREAK!

THERE'S NO TIME! COME ON! LET'S GO!

BUT I GIVE THE ORDERS AROUND HERE! NOW, TAKE A BREAK, YOU HEAR... A BREAK...

YOU TAKE A BREAK... WE'RE GOING ON!

THAT WAS A GOOD ONE, .. BY GOLLY!

I'VE GOT ONE FOR YOU TAKEN FROM MY BOOK "ACROPOLIS NOW"

HILARIOUS! THEY'LL FLIP THEIR WHIGS IN BRITANNIA!

I don't quite know how to put it in Gottic and Egyptian but it's funny there's no de-nile!...

!!!

CRAZY! THEY'RE CRAZY! THEY'RE ACTUALLY LOOKING FORWARD TO SEEING COMBAT!

PAF!

THE COLUMN OF THE 1ST LEGION 3RD COHORT, 2ND MANIPLE, 1ST CENTURY MARCHES ON. BUT THERE HAS BEEN A SLIGHT CHANGE IN MARCHING ORDER...

HALT! WE'LL SET UP CAMP HERE FOR TONIGHT!

ER UM... FINE. DIG A TRENCH AROUND THE CAMP! PUT UP A STOCKADE! PITCH YOUR TENTS AROUND YOUR CENTURION'S TENT! ORGANIZE SENTRY DUTY

DON'T LOSE YOUR BREATH! TAKE A LOOK AT THEM!

POP! POP!

!!!

THE MENU FOR THIS EVENING, GENTLEMEN: BOAR ON THE SPIT AND GÂTEAU À LA CRÈME

YES, THAT WILL DO

MAKE MINE BOAR KABOBS.

WHILE THEIR MEN ARE STUFFING THEIR MOUTHS, THE TWO ROMAN OFFICERS NIBBLE THEIR PLAIN REGULATION RATIONS IN THEIR TINY REGULATION TENT...

HONK! SCRONTCH! SLOP! SLIP! SCRITCH MIAM!

AND AFTER A SHORT NIGHT'S SLEEP

WOHAHO!

?

LINGUAE LAPSUS! THEY'VE GONE!

THE BARRACKS ARE IN THE NEW PORT. A PIECE OF ADVICE, BY JUPITER! BETTER GET READY FOR SHOW TIME. IF THEY SEE YOU LIKE THAT IN MASSILIA IT'S CURTAINS!

SOON AFTERWARDS, IN THE OFFICES OF THE COMMANDING TRIBUNE OF THE MASSILIA BARRACKS...

WHY YES! YOU'RE THE REINFORCEMENTS FROM CONDATUM... THE GALLEY IS READY. YOU HAVE PERMISSION TO BOARD. JULIUS CAESAR IS ENCAMPED NEAR THAPSUS WAITING TO ATTACK

HERE'S OUR GALLEY

LET'S SEE SOME ORDER AND DISCIPLINE! PLEASE REMAIN CALM!

CENTURION LINGUAE LAPSUS, PREPARED TO DEFEND THE CAUSE WE ALL ESPOUSE!

WHAT DID THAT MAN SAY?

BIG HAIRY EYEBROWS.

HA HA HA HA!

UH... RIGHT... WE'RE SHORT OF A FEW OARSMEN. EXERCISE WILL CALM THEM DOWN!

NOTHING WILL CALM THEM DOWN, CAPTAIN... ABSOLUTELY NOTHING!

MAKE READY TO CAST OFF!

WH... WHAT DO YOU MEAN, CAST OFF?

MOVE HER OUT!

HE SAID...

I KNOW, I KNOW, BIG HAIRY SNOUT!

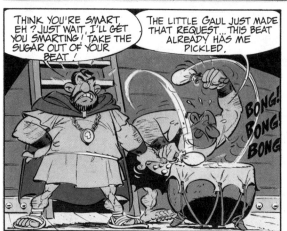

34

QUO VADIS?

WE'RE THE REINFORCEMENTS! 1ST LEGION, 3RD COHORT, 2ND MANIPLE, 1ST CENTURY!

THE CENTURION OF THE WATCH WILL SHOW YOU TO YOUR QUARTERS.

WE MUST FIND TRAGICOMIX RIGHT AWAY SO WE CAN RETURN TO GAUL AS SOON AS POSSIBLE.

RIGHT, WE'LL MAKE A SCARAB= LINE *

He says it's a lovely vacation complex.

* TODAY, WE WOULD SAY A "BEELINE".

1ST LEGION, 3RD COHORT, 2ND MANIPLE, 1ST CENTURY TAKING UP ITS QUARTERS!

IS THAT SO?! JUST WHERE IS THE 1ST LEGION, 3RD COHORT, 2ND MANIPLE, 1ST CENTURY?

?!?

THE TWO GAULS HAVE GONE TO LOOK FOR A FRIEND; THE GREEK FOUND A GAME OF CRAPS; THE BELGIAN, THE BRITON AND THE GOTH WENT TO GET A BEER; THE COOK IS LOOKING FOR THE INGREDIENTS TO MAKE CRÊPES SUZETTE AND CRISMUS BONUS HAS REPORTED SICK. MAY I BE DISMISSED NOW?

THERE, THERE, I'M SURE YOUR GIRLFRIEND WILL COME BACK TO YOU.

32

JULIUS CAESAR'S TENT ...

SCIPION, OUR ENEMY, IS HOLDING OUT TO THE NORTH; JUBA 1ST, KING OF NUMIDIA AND THE TRAITOR AFRANIUS TO THE SOUTH. SO, TO SIZE UP THE SITUATION ...

?

WHO ARE YOU? HOW DARE YOU ENTER CAESAR'S TENT?

IS THAT YOU PTIGHTNET?

WHAT'S THIS MAN SAYING?

HE, UH, HE WANTS TO KNOW IF YOU ARE A G.O. ... ONE OF THE COUNSELORS FROM THE CAMP... MASTER OF CEREMONIES... UH ...

GET OUT!

NOW, WHERE WERE WE? OUR POSITION IS SERIOUS. DO WE ATTACK ON THE NORTHERN FRONT OR...

NO, IT'S NOT A BAR. I DON'T THINK THEY'VE GOT BEER IN THERE!

TERRIBLY SORRY BUT WE SAW THIS BIG TENT AND THOUGHT THAT PERHAPS IT WAS ...

GET OUT, BY JUPITER!

THIS BATTLE MUST BE A DECISIVE VICTORY OVER MY ENEMIES IN THE CAMP OF POMPEY, AND...

IS TRAGICOMIX THERE?

WHO IN THE BLAZES ARE THESE PEOPLE?

1ST LEGION 3RD COHORT 2ND MANIPLE 1ST CENTURY, AVE!

WELL, THERE YOU ARE! THERE ARE GOING TO BE A FEW CHANGES AROUND HERE! THIS HERE IS A MILI= TARY CAMP! THAT MEANS ARMY DISCIPLINE HERE! THERE'S A GUARDHOUSE HERE! AND I KNOW SOMEONE WHO...

COMMANDING OFFICER OF THE DETACHMENT OF THE 1ST LEGION, 3RD COHORT, 2ND MANIPLE, 1ST CENTURY?

YOU'RE LOOKING AT HIM!

RIGHT, WE ARREST YOU IN THE NAME OF JULIUS CAESAR, WHO DOESN'T LIKE TO BE INTERRUP= TED WHEN HE'S TALKING! OFF TO THE GUARDHOUSE WE GO!

WE'VE LOOKED IN EVERY NOOK AND CRANNY FOR TRAGICOMIX BUT CAN'T FIND HIM ANYWHERE...

HE'S GOT TO BE SOMEWHERE IN AFRICA...

AVE, RECRUITS! SO YOU'VE COME FOR SOME HEAVY ACTION?... I COULD GIVE YOU GUYS A FEW TIPS IF THERE WAS SOME LIQUID REFRESHMENT IN IT FOR ME...

YOU SEE, I'M AN OLD VETERAN! I KNOW ALL THE ROPES! I KNOW EVERYBODY IN THESE PARTS!

BONG! BONG! BONG!

DO YOU KNOW A LEGIONARY CALLED TRAGICOMIX?

TRAGICOMIX... TRAGICOMIX WITH A T... AS IN TIMEO DANAOS ET DONA FERENTES?...

A YOUNG GUY? GOOD LOOKING?

YES THAT'S THE ONE!

HE'S NOT ALL THAT GOOD LOOKING!

POOR GUY HAD BARELY LANDED WHEN HE DISAPPEARED IN A SKIRMISH WITH SCIPIO'S MEN...

34

YOU MEAN TRAGICOMIX HAS BEEN...

PERHAPS NOT. SOMETIMES THEY TAKE PRISONERS FOR INTERROGATION.

KGB MIGHT POSSIBLY HAVE SOME MORE INFORMATION FOR YOU WHEN HE RETURNS.

KGB?

YES, HE'S OUR CRACK SPY! HE WENT TO SEE WHAT'S DOING IN SCIPIO'S CAMP. WE EXPECT HIM BACK TONIGHT. I'LL BRING HIM AROUND. HE'S A BUDDY OF MINE.

WHAT A STRANGE NAME, KGB.

THAT'S HIS CODE NAME. HIS REAL NAME IS BOLSHEVIX... NOW, WHAT ABOUT THAT DRINK?

GO OVER TO OUR COOK'S TENT...

TELL HIM WE SENT YOU.

THANKS, GUYS! SEE YOU TONIGHT!

THAT NIGHT OUTSIDE THE CAMP GATES...

KGB

WHAT'S THE PASSWORD?

DIGNUS EST INTRARE.

YOU MAY PASS.

CAESAR'S EXPECTING YOU KGB.

SCIPIO IS PREPARING HIS ATTACK, O CAESAR. HIS ARMY IS POWERFUL!

HMM... I OUGHT TO ATTACK FIRST, BUT I'M JUST NOT SURE...

SOME ROOKIES WANT TO SEE YOU KGB. WAIT TILL YOU SEE THEIR WINE LAKE! IT'S UNREAL!

LET'S GET GOING CHERRI LIQUORUS.

HEY, ASTERIX, I'D GIVE ANYTHING TO SEE THE SENTRY'S FACE WHEN HE SEES THAT YOU BROKE DOWN HIS GATE!

SO, WHERE ARE THESE LEGIONARIES WHO WANT TO GO FOR AN EVENING STROLL IN THE DESERT WITHOUT A PASS?

THEY... THEY'VE GONE! THEY'VE DESTROYED THE GATE!

RING THE ALARM! THEY MUST BE SCIPIO'S SPIES! I'LL GO AND TELL CAESAR!

SOON AFTERWARDS...

THESE MEN MUST BE CAPTURED BEFORE THEY REACH THE ENEMY!

PAF!

BONG!

BUT OUR FRIENDS HAVE NEARLY REACHED THE ENEMY ALREADY... SPECIFI= CALLY A PATROL SQUAD FROM SCIPIO'S ARMY...

TWO ROMANS!

SO? IT DOESN'T MEAN A THING. WE'RE ROMANS TOO!

THAT'S THE NASTY THING ABOUT THESE CIVIL WARS...

OH NO, NOT ANOTHER VOICE CRYING IN THE WILDERNESS...

HEY! YOU TWO! WHAT'S THE PASSWORD?

DON'T TELL ME YOU DON'T KNOW THE PASSWORD!

I'M SURE I DO! COGITO, ERGO SUM.

FINE! YOU MAY PASS.

THANKS. COME ALONG NOW BOYS!

HEY! WAIT A SECOND! JUST WHAT DO YOU THINK YOU'RE DOING?

CHARGE! CHARGE!

YOU SEE TO THE OTHERS, OBELIX!

WHAT ARE YOU WAITING FOR?... CHARGE!

BIFF!

AND CLOSE BY WE FIND ONE OF CAESAR'S PATROLS HOT ON THE HEELS OF OUR GAULISH FRIENDS...

CHARGE! CHARGE!

LISTEN! SCIPIO'S ATTACKING!

WE MUST RETURN AND TELL CAESAR!

YES, LET'S GO BACK!

AND SNAPPY!

42

43

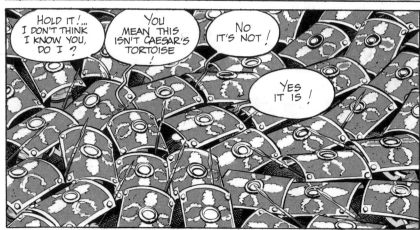

44

LET'S GET OUR THINGS IN CAESAR'S CAMP AND RETURN TO GAUL.

EVERYTHING SEEMS EASY AS PIE WITH YOU!

THAT'S BECAUSE WE'VE GOT SMARTS.

SOON AFTERWARDS...

HOW IS MY BELOVED LITTLE PHILHARMONIA?

SHE'S FINE!

LOOK! CAESAR'S ARMY IS COMING BACK!

WHAT SHOULD WE DO NOW?

WHAT SHOULD WE DO...?

WE CHARGE BY TOUTATIS!

OBELIX!

YOU... YOU'RE BEING PAGED!...

CRRAAASH!

WHAT'S UP?

THERE'S NO NEED TO GET CARRIED AWAY. HERE COMES JULIUS CAESAR.

IT SEEMS TO ME WE'VE ALREADY MET, GAULS. WHO ARE YOU?

OBELIX AND ASTERIX!

1ST LEGION, 3RD COHORT AND I FORGET THE REST.

WE ENLISTED IN YOUR ARMY TO BRING TRAGICOMIX BACK TO PHILHARMONIA.

46

AND WHILE THE ROMAN GALLEY CARRIES OUR FRIENDS TOWARDS THE HALCYON SHORES OF GAUL, YET ANOTHER ENEMY IS LURKING AT SEA, WATCHING AND WAITING...

LUCKY FOR US WE MANAGED TO BUY THIS SHIP FROM THE PHOENICIANS WHO FOUND US FLOATING ON THE RAFT... BUT IT COST AN ARM AND A LEG... WE HAVE TO PAY IT OFF QUICKLY...

SHIP STRAIGHT AHEAD, CAP'N!

SWELL! THAT WILL KEEP US AFLOAT!

GO TO IT, MATES! HIP, HIP...

HURRAY!

AT LAST, AFTER A RELATIVELY UNEVENT= FUL VOYAGE, OUR FRIENDS RETURN TRIUM= PHANT TO THE GAULISH VILLAGE...

PHILHARMONIA!

DOGMATIX!

THANK YOU! THANK YOU! HOW CAN I EVER THANK YOU?

OH, T'WAS NOTHING...

NOTHING? YOU MUST BE KIDDING! YOU SHOULD HAVE SEEN THEM PHILHARMONIA! THEY WERE GREAT! SUPERB! AND OBELIX! HE TOOK ON CAESAR'S ENTIRE ARMY SINGLE HANDEDLY.

OH WELL IT WAS JUST A SMALL ARMY, NOT MUCH AT ALL ...

A VERITABLE POWERHOUSE! A TORNADO!

THANK YOU, OBELIX!

NOTHING CAN STOP HIM! NOTHING CAN KNOCK HIM OFF HIS FEET! NOTHING...

BOOM!

? ? ? ?

WELL, WE'RE ON OUR WAY...

WHAT, YOU'RE NOT STAYING FOR THE BANQUET?

NO, WE'RE OFF TO CONDATUM TO GET MARRIED.

GOOD-BYE AND THANKS AGAIN, ASTERIX!

AND NOW THAT OBELIX HAS REGAINED HIS GOOD SPIRITS, HIS HEARTY APPETITE, HIS DARLING BOARS AND DOGMATIX, ALL OUR FRIENDS ARE REUNITED AT AN OFFICIAL BANQUET... WELL, ALMOST ALL...

WOOF!

?!?!

UDERZO & GOSCINNY

THE END.